The Littles Get Trapped!

The Littles
Get Trapped!

Adapted by **Teddy Slater**
from **THE LITTLES AND THE BIG STORM**
by **John Peterson**
Illustrated by **Jacqueline Rogers**

SCHOLASTIC INC.
New York   Toronto   London   Auckland   Sydney
Mexico City   New Delhi   Hong Kong

"MmmRRROW!"

the Biggs' cat roared.

At least it sounded that way

to Lucy Little's tiny ears.

"Poor Hildy," Lucy said
to her brother, Tom.
"She hasn't had a bite to eat
since the Biggs went on
vacation two days ago."

The Littles were only a few
inches tall, and they had long,
beautiful tails.
The whole family
lived inside the walls of
the Biggs' house—
but the Biggs didn't know it.

When the Biggs were home, the
Littles stayed hidden.
But now the Biggs were away.
The Littles could come and go
in the house as they pleased.
There was only one problem....

The boy next door had
promised to feed Hildy,
but he had not shown up.
"Why don't we feed her?"
Tom suggested.

"The cat food is in the refrigerator,"

Lucy said.

"The door is too heavy for us to open."

But Tom would not give up.

Hildy was his special friend.

Tom finally came up

with the perfect plan.

He tied one end of the rope

to Hildy's collar.

He tied the other end

to the refrigerator door handle.

Meanwhile, Lucy tied a

thin string to a catnip mouse.

Then she hid behind the

living room door.

When Tom yelled, "Now!"

Lucy pulled the string

with all her might.

The catnip mouse scooted
across the floor...

...and Hildy scooted after it.

C-r-e-e-a-k!

The refrigerator door

opened just a little bit.

But that was enough.

Tom and Lucy jammed a
cereal box into the opening.
Then they untied the rope
and set Hildy free.

The Little children climbed
into the refrigerator.
The bottom shelf was full
of fruits and vegetables.
But there was no cat food.

Lucy pulled herself up

to the next shelf.

Behind the milk and eggs

she saw the cat food.

"Look!" said Lucy.

"Listen!" Tom said at the same time.

A soft scratching noise was

coming from the front hall.

It sounded like a key in a lock.

"Uh-oh!" Tom said.

"Let's get out of here."

But it was too late....

Someone was already

in the kitchen.

"Here, kitty, kitty,"

a boy's voice called.

"It's time for lunch."

Footsteps marched toward

the refrigerator.

The Littles hid.

The footsteps stopped.

"How did this box get here?"

the boy said. He kicked it away.

Tom peeked out and saw
a huge hand coming
toward him.
Quickly, he backed up...

...right into a bowl of Jell-O.

Splat!

The boy picked up

the cat food and slammed

the refrigerator door shut.

"Tom! Where are you?"

Lucy cried.

"What happened to the light?"

"It goes out when the door

is shut," Tom told her.

"Don't worry," he added.

"I have a candle.

I'll light it as soon as

I get out of this mess."

Lucy looked around the icy
refrigerator and shivered.
"Oh, Tom," she wailed.
"We're locked in!
What are we going to do?"

"There's only one thing

we can do," Tom said.

"Help!" he shouted.

"Help!" Lucy shouted.

"HELP!" they shouted together.

Suddenly, the refrigerator door
opened, and the light
came on again.

"Tom! Lucy!" Mr. Little called.

"Daddy!" Tom and Lucy cried.

Mr. Little helped Lucy
out of the refrigerator.

"How did you know we were
in here?" she asked.

"How did you get the door
open?" Tom asked.

"Uncle Pete and I saw
what happened," Mr. Little explained.
"We waited for the boy to leave.
Then we used this ruler to
pry the door open."

Mr. Little gave Tom
and Lucy a big hug.
"The refrigerator is a
dangerous place," he said.
"You must never go
in there again."

"We won't," Lucy promised.

"But do you know what happens

when the door is closed?"

she went on.

"The light goes out,

that's what!"